The Ex Games

Part I

J. S. Cooper & Helen Cooper

This book is a work of fiction. Any resemblance to actual persons, living or dead, or actual events is entirely coincidental. Names, characters, businesses, organizations, places, events, and incidents are the product of the author's imagination or are used fictitiously.

Table of Contents

Chapter 1

"It's one weekend, Katie. You'll survive." Meg giggled at the expression on my face. "I mean, it can't be that bad…can it?"
"It's going to be worse than bad," I groaned and flopped down on her bed. "I may die. I mean it. I may literally die of embarrassment."
"You won't die. You may be embarrassed though." She gave me a sympathetic smile.
"I can't believe this is happening to me." I buried my head in her pillow. "Of all the jobs in all of the world, I had to get this one."
"You were happy about it a few weeks ago."
"That was before I heard about this weekend training." I groaned and stared up at her. "I had no idea he worked for Marathon Corp."
"Well, he more than works for them now." She laughed, and I shuddered.
"I should quit. I'm going to quit!" I cried out melodramatically. "You'll have to take care of the rent for the next few months while I look for a job. I'll cook and clean and be your house woman."
"Yeah, right. You can't cook or clean for shit." Meg collapsed next to me onto the bed and rubbed my shoulder. "And you know I'm saving up for my trip."
"You're not really going to travel around the world and leave me, are you?"
"You can always come with me."
"But I have a job," I whined and saw her grinning at me. "Fine, I'm not quitting. This is the job I've been waiting for my whole life. I'm not quitting just because he owns the company."
"Hear ye, hear ye."
"Don't go being a lawyer on me," I moaned at her, and she laughed.
"I didn't go through three years of law school to just stop." She jumped up off the bed and grabbed my hands. "Come

on, lazy bones. Let's go shopping. You may as well look hot when you see him."

"I don't want to see him. Maybe he'll have forgotten me." The thought sent a ripple of hurt through me.

"There's no way he will have forgotten you."

"He's going to hate me." I gave her a pained expression. "Or he's going to fire me."

"He dumped you. He's not going to hate you." Meg brushed her long blonde hair as she waited for me to get up. "And we're going to make him regret it."

"Why oh why did Brandon Hastings have to buy Marathon Corp?" I slowly dragged myself off of the bed and looked into the vanity mirror. I wasn't altogether displeased with my appearance, but I wished I didn't look quite so washed out. My long brown hair looked messy, but that was nothing a brush couldn't fix. I examined my face and was pleased that my brown eyes looked bright and cheerful even though I was filled with inner turmoil.

"You look gorgeous, Katie."

"I look like a little kid," I groaned. "I don't look like a manager."

"Hey, it's not your fault you're super smart. So what if you're twenty-five and an executive manager already? Anyone who cares about that is just jealous."

"Brandon will care." I sighed and I bit my lower lip as I grew serious and put my face in my hands. "Oh my God, Meg, what am I going to do?"

"It's all in the past, Katie. You made a mistake. He can't be holding a grudge for all these years."

"It was a pretty big mistake." I made a face. "Some may even say it was a lie."

"Well, it was a lie." Meg made an apologetic face as she spoke honestly. "But it was seven years ago."

"Yeah." I straightened my shirt and pushed my shoulders back like my mother had taught me. "I'm sure he's not thinking about some silly girl he dated seven years ago."

"You were eighteen, new to love! These things happen."

"Yeah." I nodded in agreement. "If he had half a brain, he would have figured it out."
"Exactly." Meg linked her arm through mine and we walked to the living room. "He's the one that broke your heart."
"Exactly." My heart beat slowly as I remembered the tears I had cried late at night. I had been devastated when Brandon dumped me right before Christmas in the first semester of my first college year. Absolutely devastated. I hadn't been able to sleep or eat for weeks. He had made my second semester of college absolutely awful. It wasn't until the summer and a trip to London with my parents that I was finally able to accept that what we'd had was forever gone. He had been my first lover and my first love, but to him, I was just a little girl playing around in fairytale land.

***

Flying in first class was a perk of my job that I loved, even though this was the only time I had actually traveled first class. I sat back in the wide leather seat and looked out the window, trying to lose my thoughts in the clouds. I felt worried as I tried to relax and thought about what was going to happen this weekend. I had only been working for Marathon Corp for about a month. It was the first job that made me feel like a real professional, and I felt like I was going to be fired already.
I was in charge of the whole New England area, and I knew that most, if not all, of the lower managers below me felt that I wasn't qualified for the job. I myself had been amazed when I had been hired as an executive manager. I knew I had the degrees for the job—marketing BA from Columbia and a business management master's degree from NYU. But I didn't have that much experience—only the summer internships I'd done while getting my master's. But I had brains and verve and a lot of initiative. And I knew that I was good at my job. However, I knew that there was no way in hell Brandon would allow me to stay if he realized who I was.

I mean, there was a chance he wouldn't recognize me. It had been seven years, and we had only dated for five months. It had been the best five months of my life, but for him, I bet it was nothing. I also knew that I looked more mature now and definitely dressed like a woman who knew the world. My usually wavy brown hair was flat-ironed straight and I had on mascara and eye shadow. I looked nothing like the girl I'd been when I started college.

Then I had been bright eyed, with minimal makeup and no hair products taming my normally wild hair. Thinking back, it should have been obvious to Brandon that I had been lying, but I knew it was hardly his fault that I had deceived him. I hadn't meant to. It had just been one white lie. I hadn't expected him to ask me out. I hadn't expected to fall in love with him.

I sighed as I remembered the first time I saw Brandon Hastings outside the bar. That night was one of the best in my life. Meg and some other girls had convinced me to join them at a bar in the Lower East Side that they knew didn't card minors if they wore short enough skirts and red enough lipstick. I remembered the day clearly. It was a beautiful, warm August day, not too hot, and we were all excited to be starting college. None of us had lived in New York before, and we were all pretty naïve and green. I don't think that any of us had really had boyfriends in high school because we'd all been too busy studying, trying to earn our way into an Ivy League school. And it had paid off for all of us—we were incoming freshmen at Columbia University, and I think the giddiness that had taken over our lives came to fruition that night.

It was a Friday, the weekend before orientation classes were going to start, so one of the girls had the bright idea of christening our first week before classes started. I had never had any alcohol before and was as eager as the rest to go out and party. We were in New York, so why shouldn't we party it up? We'd all dressed up in the shortest skirts and the tightest tops we owned. I'd borrowed high heels from Meg and a bunch of makeup, and we took the 1 train to 42nd Street and then caught a cab to Doug's.

Doug's was everything I had imagined it was going to be: dark and musty, with bright lights and lots of cool-looking people. I was amazed that we had been able to walk right in without even a second glance from the bouncer. Our plan had worked. None of us were carded, and we walked quickly to the bar to get some drinks. Felicity, who was the one who told us about the bar, ordered us our first round of drinks. Scotch on the rocks. It tasted awful, and I thought my stomach was on fire as it burned slightly.

"That's just to get us buzzed faster," she grinned before ordering a round of Sex on the Beaches. "These will taste better, girls."

And she had been right. I guzzled two glasses down within half an hour, not thinking anything of it, as they hadn't tasted alcoholic at all. We were all just standing around when the DJ started playing some old Madonna songs and Meg grabbed my hand and we ran to the dance floor, giggling. The other girls followed quickly and we danced around as if we were on *Dancing With The Stars*.

We danced all night, and even though different guys came up to us, we turned them down. That wasn't a night for us to look for guys, but a night for us to bond with each other. It was the first of many memories we were going to make together.

We stumbled out of the bar at about one a.m. I remember that Meg and Felicity went to look for a cab while the other girls went to the bathroom. I stood there waiting outside the club and leaning against the wall, feeling dizzy and sick. The evening air was cool, and I shivered in my lack of clothing.

"Are you okay?" The voice was deep and husky, and I remember feeling comforted even though I hadn't been able to look up. "Do you need me to take you somewhere?" The voice was closer this time, and I felt warm hands on my shoulders as he forced me to look up at him.

"I'm fine." I giggled and looked up at him through my fake eyelashes. "Just waiting on my friends."
"You're drunk." He frowned and looked around. "It looks like your friends have left you."
"No, they're in the ladies' room." I pointed toward Doug's. "I'm just waiting on them to come out.
"I see." He stared down at me and there was concern in his blue eyes. "I'll wait with you."
"Thank you." I smiled at him and then started laughing.
"What's so funny?" He frowned as he looked at me and I pointed at his face. "My face is funny?" He gave me a wry smile and I shook my head.
"You look like Clark Gable."
"You think so?"
"Yes." I grinned at him. "You're handsome."
"Why, thank you." He looked at his watch then back at me. "We will give your friends a few minutes then see about getting you home."
"Are you trying to seduce me?" I wiggled my eyebrows at him and giggled. He was handsome and I was enjoying flirting with him. His blue eyes were bright and had a wise look. His hair was jet black and contrasted well with his olive skin. He was tall and muscular and smelled like some expensive cologne I didn't know the name of. It certainly wasn't the same cologne my dad or any of my high school boy friends used.
"No, dear." He shook his head. "I don't take advantage of young women."
"You wouldn't be taking advantage of me." I licked my lips slowly. I'd read an article in Cosmopolitan that said the way to seduce a guy was to show him your tongue. "I'm twenty-two. I make my own decisions," I lied easily.
"Well, maybe we can go out when you're sober, and if you still want me to seduce you then, I'll see what I can do." He put his arm around me and his fingers felt like heaven against my skin. "You're cold. Why don't you have a coat?"
"I didn't realize how cold it would get."

"You girls these days don't know how to take care of yourselves." He looked at me disapprovingly, and I wondered how old he was. He definitely wasn't a college student like me. There was no boyish look to him. He was all man, and 100% hunk at that.

"I don't feel good." All of a sudden my head felt like it was going to explode and my stomach was swirling like a hurricane.

"My apartment is just a couple of blocks down if you want to come."

"I don't know," I mumbled as I grabbed his arm. I didn't want to think about anything. I just wanted to lie down on something cool and rest my head so the world would stop spinning.

"Come. I won't hurt you." He took my hand, and I followed him to his apartment. I know, I know—I was a dumbass. If I hadn't been drunk, I would have told him where to get off, but I wasn't in my right mind. I always thought that if only I hadn't been drunk that night, everything might have been different.

I don't really remember much of what happened later that night. It's all a blur in my mind. The next thing I remember after leaving with him is waking up in a king-sized bed, feeling like someone was banging nails into my head.

"Good morning, sunshine," a deep, warm voice greeted me, and I looked up to see him staring down at me with a cup of tea in his hand. "Drink this. I'm cooking breakfast for you right now. Lots of bacon and eggs."

"Ugh, don't talk about food," I groaned and lay back down, my brain racing a million miles a minute. Who was the gorgeous man next to me, and what was I doing in his bed?

"I'm Brandon, by the way." He smiled at me gently. "We didn't exchange names last night."

"Oh." I peeked up at him and swallowed hard. He was gorgeous, and even though I felt like death warmed up, I was still attracted to him.

"And your name is?"

"Oh, sorry. I'm Katie."

"Nice name." He smiled at me again. "Rest a little and I'll be back."
"Okay, thanks." I gave him a quick smile, lay back, and closed my eyes. *Oh my God, oh my God, have I been kidnapped?* I peeked under the sheets and groaned as I saw myself wearing only my bra and panties. He'd taken off my clothes. Then panic hit me—had we had sex? *Oh, God, did I have sex for the first time and not even know it?*
"Scrambled eggs, bacon, and lots of buttered white toast." He walked back into the room. "Nothing healthy, but it will help your hangover."
"I feel like shit," I blurted out and blushed when I realized what I'd said.
"Not surprising." He laughed. "First hangover?"
"Yeah." I nodded and felt my face going red. Did he know it was the first time I'd ever had a drink as well?
"I don't know many people who've reached the age of twenty-two and never had a drink."
"Oh?" I looked down at the plate and swallowed hard. *Should I tell him the truth?*
"Were you and your friends celebrating something?"
"Yes. Yes we were."
"Oh?" He looked at me expectantly, waiting for an answer. I knew there was no way in hell that I could tell him that we were celebrating starting college. Then the questions would start, the 'Why were you drinking?' and 'Why are you so irresponsible?' I stared at him guiltily. I felt bad and disappointed in myself. I knew that my parents back home in Florida would be upset if they knew I was already making bad choices.
"Sorry, I feel a little sick." I turned my face away from him as I felt myself becoming hypnotized by his blue eyes.
"Do you need to go to the bathroom?"
"Huh?"
"To throw up?"
"Oh, no, no." I shook my head and groaned. "I just need to lie down again."

"Sure. Feel free." He sat next to me on the bed. "Do you mind if I lie down next to you?"

"No," I whispered. My heart was beating fast again and little men were jumping around in my stomach.

"Are you new to the city?"

"Yeah, I moved here from Florida a few weeks ago, for, uh, a job." Technically I wasn't lying. I was going to college to get a job.

"Oh nice. Where are you working?"

"Ooh, my head," I groaned and rolled over, trying to control my panicked breathing. I hated lying and was already regretting my comments. I felt his hand rubbing my back and I froze. What was he doing?

"You're very trusting to be here with me, Katie. I'm not sure where in Florida you're from, but there are a lot of wolves in New York, and they are looking to prey on young girls in their twenties like you."

"I can take care of myself," I mumbled and turned over.

"You're lucky I'm a nice guy." He chuckled, and I looked up at him, not sure if he was joking or being serious. He looked even more handsome close up. His blue eyes were shrewd, and I felt like he could see right through me.

"Yes, thank you."

"I could kiss you right now." His voice sounded like a growl, and my eyes widened. "Don't worry, sweet thing. I'll let you get better first."

"First?" I swallowed.

"That's if you don't have anything against men in their thirties?"

"No, no, of course not," I squeaked out. Thirty wasn't that old. I mean, he wasn't old enough to be my dad.

"Good. I don't normally go for girls in their twenties, but you seem different." His eyes crinkled and he laughed. "That is, if you let me take you on a date."

"You want to take me on a date?" I stammered in shock. Was I dreaming? This seriously good-looking man wanted to take me out?

"I think you're someone I want to get to know better, Katie." He nodded as he looked at me seriously.
"Thank you," I mumbled with a wide smile. I didn't bother to hide my excitement from him. I didn't know then that you aren't supposed to let a guy know that you have feelings for him.
"You're welcome, my dear. You're very welcome." He jumped off of the bed then and grabbed the plate. "Try and get some more sleep, and we'll see how you feel when you wake up."
"Okay." I nodded sleepily and closed my eyes again. Sleep found me easily and I stretched in the luxurious bed, imagining Brandon's lips kissing me softly.

***

"Ma'am, would you like anything else to drink?" The flight attendant tapped me on the arm and I broke out of my reverie.
"No, thanks." I smiled at her and rubbed my forehead. I was starting to get a headache and a small heartache as well. I hated remembering the first days after I met Brandon because he had been so sweet and wonderful. He had been a man I'd thought only existed in romance novels. The beginning of our relationship was magical. It was only the end that was the stuff that nightmares are made of.
"Okay, just let me know if you change your mind."
"Thanks." I smiled. "Do you know how many more hours until we land in San Francisco?"
"It'll be about two more hours, Ms. Raymond."
"Thanks." I looked back out the window and thought about Brandon again. Maybe I wouldn't even see him. I'm sure he will be busy with the board of directors. What time will he have for a manager? It was just my luck that he had bought the company I worked for. Out of all the companies in the world, he'd had to pick mine. What sort of bad luck was that? He was going to fire me, I just knew it. He would take one look at me, laugh in my face, and fire me. Maybe after calling

me a liar. And what could I say? What would I tell HR? I knew the answer to that. I would just leave with my tail between my legs. Because it would be true. I had lied to him. At first, I'd had a reason, but then I had built up the lie, making everything more complicated. And then it had all exploded in my face. I closed my eyes again and thought of Brandon—my sexy, hunky Brandon.

***

"How was your day today?" His voice was warm and I smiled into the phone.
"Good, what about yours?"
"Long." He groaned. "I don't want to talk about it. I'd rather talk about our dinner tomorrow night. Are you excited?"
"Yes!" I exclaimed in excitement.
"I love that you don't hide your true emotions. I've dated way too many women in New York who act like they can't stand me."
"That's silly," I said honestly.
Thinking back, he should have realized the truth from our phone calls. Brandon had taken my number before putting me in a cab home the afternoon after he had taken me home. He had wanted me to spend the weekend with him, but I'd known that I had to get back to the dorms or my friends would be mad. He had called me every night since then, and I'd delighted in his phone calls.
He'd made me laugh and feel special. He seemed to really want to know how I was spending my days, and he told me little things about himself as well. He was the only son of a billionaire banker and worked at his father's hedge fund. He hated his job but knew that it was his duty. He owned his apartment in Chelsea, and he had a house in the Hamptons and an apartment in San Francisco. He preferred the West Coast but had to stay on the East Coast due to work. He loved dogs but traveled so much that he thought it was unfair to have one. He loved Mexican food and jazz and collecting first-edition books. He was also thirty-five. When he first told

me that, I'd felt my heart stop beating. Thirty-five sounded so much older than me. Thirty-five was old enough to be my dad, if he'd had sex at a young age. Thirty-five made me feel guilty for having him think I was twenty-two, about to turn twenty-three. Thirty-five made me keep my real age a secret. I didn't want to stop talking to him. I didn't want his calls to end, and I very much wanted to go on that dinner date with him. Thirty-five made me realize that I couldn't let him know that I was eighteen, even though I very much wanted to be honest about my age.

"I can't wait to see you tomorrow," he whispered into the phone. "I'm going to take you to dinner and then we can go dancing if you want."

"That would be nice. Do you know what club you're thinking of?" I grabbed my laptop so I could check Yelp to see if they let in people under twenty-one.

"Oh, not a club." He smiled. "I was thinking we could go to some salsa classes."

"Salsa?"

"Yes, you know, the Spanish dance."

"Oh, yeah. I've just never heard of a date where people went to classes."

"What are you used to, Katie? Burgers and movies?"

"Something like that." I laughed.

"Then that just means you've been dating boys, not men like me."

"Yeah, that could be right." If he'd only known just how true his words were.

"Men in their twenties are still chasing the almighty dollar and trying to get laid. Men in their thirties know that money and sex are not important."

"It's not?" I'd had neither and still hoped for both.

"I mean, we need it to live, of course. But it's not worth losing your life for either."

"I suppose that's true."

"So tomorrow, shall I pick you up from your apartment?"

"My apartment?" My body burned as I stared at my roommate's empty bed. "Uh, no. I've got a late day at work

tomorrow. I can meet you at the restaurant." I couldn't believe how easily the lies slid from my mouth.
"Okay, that makes sense." He yawned. "Tomorrow will be our first date."
"I know."
"I can't wait to see you again." He chuckled. "And if anyone I knew heard me say that, they'd think someone had stolen my body."
"Why?"
"This isn't me, Katie. I'm not a romantic guy. I don't do relationships."
"Oh, I didn't know." I felt disappointed and confused. "Why are you talking to me then?"
"I don't know. I guess there was something about you that touched me as I walked by."
"You mean my puke?" I joked and he laughed.
"Thank God, no." He cleared his throat. "I'm not really sure why I stopped and took you home though. I've asked myself several times what I was thinking. You could have been a psycho."
"*I* could have been a psycho? *You* could have been a psycho."
"I'm glad neither of us is a psycho."
"Me too. Sweet dreams, Brandon."
"Sweet dreams, Katie."
"Have a good day at work."
"You too."
"Thanks." *I'll be doing the assignment I didn't do tonight because I was waiting for your call.*
"I'll see you tomorrow."
"See you then." And then we hung up. I lay in my bed and hugged my pillow tightly. I was so excited. This was going to be my first proper date and it was with a man who knew the world, and he was interested in *me*. I couldn't believe it. I was worried about what we would talk about. What if I sounded like an idiot?
"You up?" The door creaked and Meg walked in with a handful of books.

"Yeah." I sat up and looked at her with a guilty pang. I hadn't studied all week. It was only the first week, but I knew I had to keep up or I was going to fail out. Everyone in my class at Columbia was smart, and they all seemed to know more than I did. There was no way I was going to be able to sail through my classes without studying like I had in high school.

"How was Mr. Wonderful?" She giggled as she sat her books down on the desk and then pulled out her pajamas.

"He wants to take me salsa dancing."

"But you don't know how to salsa." She frowned as she pulled off her t-shirt and then slipped on her nightgown.

"I know, but he's taking us to classes."

"Wow." She looked impressed and the fell on top of her bed. "I'm so tired."

"Aww." I gave her a sympathetic look. "You don't have to go hardcore right away."

"I do. I need to get a 4.0 GPA if I want to get into Harvard or Yale Law."

"We just started undergrad, Meg." I giggled.

"I know that. You know that. But does Brandon Hastings know that as yet?"

"No," I groaned and lay staring at the ceiling. "I can't tell him, Meg. Not yet. He won't want to see me if he knows I'm eighteen."

"You never know."

"Trust me, I know. He's working on Wall Street, living in a swanky apartment, and I've just started college living in the dorms with a roommate in single beds." My stomach tightened in knots. "He wouldn't give me the time of day if he knew."

"You're still you. He'll still like you."

"No, he won't. He'll think I'm a kid."

"I don't know, Katie. I just have a bad feeling he's going to figure out you're not twenty-two."

"I'll tell him eventually," I sighed. "Once we get to know each other better. I'll tell him then."

"Okay." She yawned. "Shit, I'm tired. I'm falling asleep already."

"Sweet dreams, Meg."

And in response, she started snoring.

The next day was crazy. Meg lent me one of her dresses and another pair of heels, and I walked to the station on 116th with a huge grin on my face. I knew I looked good because I had caught several guys eyeing me as I walked down Broadway. I was so excited I thought I was going to throw up. I was going on a date with a hot man—a very hot man—and all I wanted to do was sing and smile. I changed trains in Herald Square and then looked on my phone for the best directions to get to the restaurant. I got a little lost and ended up arriving about ten minutes late. I saw Brandon waiting outside for me and his eyes lit up as I ran over to him quickly.

"Sorry," I gasped, slightly out of breath. "I can't walk fast in these heels."

"You should have caught a cab."

"I, uh, prefer the train. It's more environmentally friendly," I lied. I only had a thousand dollars to last me a few months and I certainly wasn't going to waste it on cabs.

"I do like a girl that thinks of the environment."

"That's me."

"I thought you were going to stand me up." His blue eyes sparkled as he surveyed my appearance. I looked him over hungrily. He looked even more handsome than I had remembered, with a crisp light blue shirt that illuminated his eyes and a pair of grey slacks. He had on flat black leather shoes that looked expensive and shiny.

"Oh, sorry. I got a little lost." I made a face and he laughed before reaching over and kissed me lightly. I stood there looking at him stupidly, and he laughed and ran his hands through his hair.

"Sorry, I've been waiting to kiss you for a week."

"No need to apologize. I liked it."

"You're always so honest. I love it."

"I try." I smiled back weakly, thinking about the big lie I was keeping from him.
"We can skip dinner if you want." He leaned in toward me and I could feel the warmth of his skin even though he wasn't touching me.
"Oh? You want to go straight to the salsa classes?" I asked stupidly.
"No, I was thinking we could go back to my place."
"Your place?" I stared at him for a moment before it clicked. "Oh. Oh." I blushed and bit my lower lip as I wondered what to say. "I don't have sex on the first date," I finally blurted out. "I'm not a prude or anything, but I've always thought that—"
"No need to explain." He grabbed my hand. "I respect your want to wait. It will make it more special."
"Exactly." I nodded in agreement and walked with him into the restaurant.
"How was work today, Katie?"
"Uh, pretty good. You?"
"It was the same. Only it wasn't as bad, as I knew I was going to see you this evening."
"That's sweet." I blushed. "I thought about you today as well."
"I guess that's a sign."
"Sign of what?"
"That we're meant to be." He winked at me and I felt my heart explode in happiness. This was a man who knew how to worm his way into a woman's heart.

***

"Ladies and gentlemen, we're approaching San Francisco International Airport. We should be landing in about thirty minutes. Please put your seats in the upright position." The captain's words diverted me from my memories again. I made sure my seat was upright and my seatbelt tightened as I smiled at the memories of that first weekend. I had stayed the whole weekend at Brandon's apartment and we had stayed up all of Friday night watching French movies on Netflix. Then on Saturday he had taken me into Brooklyn and we'd had brunch at a cute little place in Park Slope. It had been perfect. He hadn't even tried to touch me. Just two long, intense kisses before bed and then he'd fallen asleep while I lay there staring at his back, wanting to touch him and feel his skin next to mine. Only I'd been too scared and pathetic. I'd still been a girl pretending to be a woman.

Chapter 2

"Welcome to the Diva Hotel, Mrs. Raymond."
"Ms." I smiled at the front desk clerk. "It's Ms."
"Sorry, Ms. Raymond. Would you prefer two full size beds or one king?"
"King, please." I handed her my credit card for incidentals and waited for my room key.
"Is there anything else we can help you with today?"
"No, that's all, thanks." I took my credit card back, grabbed my suitcase, and walked over to the elevator. I saw a doorway to my left that led to a Starbucks, and I figured I could grab a coffee there in the morning before the orientation started. I was going to need to be as alert as possible as soon as I arrived. I walked into the elevator with its fluorescent purple lights and was immediately taken back to the night I had convinced Brandon to go to a nightclub with me. It had been the second week we had been seeing each other. We'd gone out to dinner and were walking back to his place when we passed Doug's. I'd grabbed his arm and stopped him.
"Let's go in." I grinned and nodded toward the door. The strobe lights and booming top-40 music crept through the doorway and he shuddered. "Come on, it'll be fun."
"I don't do clubs." He shook his head with a small smile.
"Just for five minutes."
"I guess I could do five minutes." He grabbed my hand and we walked in easily without being carded, just as I thought. I wasn't dumb this time, and we bypassed the bar, going straight to the dance floor. I grabbed his hands and started dancing. At first, he was a bit stiff. I could tell that he wasn't one for bumping and grinding, but he seemed to get into the swing of things very quickly. One of my favorite rap songs came on, and I pushed back against him excitedly. He seemed to enjoy it and allowed his hands to roam freely over my stomach and all the way up to the underside of my breasts as he held on to me.

I could remember the next moment clearly. A purple strobe light illuminated us in the room and we danced slowly in the crowd of people. I laughed and shimmied, enjoying the vitality I felt in the room. Then his hands slid all the way up, and I felt them cupping my breasts as we danced. I paused for a split second, startled by the feel of his hands kneading my breasts. It felt different and it felt good. I looked around quickly to see if anyone had noticed, but no one was paying attention to us. They were too caught up in what they were doing.

Doug's was filled with people, but in that moment, as the beat ruined our hearing and our bodies moved together as one, it felt like we were all alone and my body felt like it was on fire. His fingers became more aggressive against my breasts, and as he pinched my nipples, I backed into him hard, crying out in pleasure, though the sound was muffled by the music around us.

Brandon pulled me around and into him, and then his lips came crashing down on mine. I kissed him back eagerly, my tongue entering his mouth and exploring every part. I sucked on his tongue eagerly, enjoying the faint taste of chocolate from the shared dessert we'd had at the restaurant. His hands lowered from my back to my ass, and he cupped my ass cheeks as he pushed me into him. I gasped against his mouth as I felt something hard pressing against my belly. I knew without a doubt that it was his erection, and a secret thrill ran from the tips of my toes, up my legs, through my belly, to my tingling breasts, and into my eager mouth. I had done that to him. I had turned him on and he wanted me. It made me feel heady with power. Here was this handsome, rich, and captivating man, and he wanted me. Even though I didn't have a lot of experience and I didn't dress in fancy clothes or know how to apply makeup. Even though I talked about movies too much and rambled on about poets and writers late into the night. He still wanted me.

I kissed him back harder then, pushing myself into him, running my hands through his hair. I was caught up in the moment as I ravished him harder than he'd ravished me.

Sometimes I thought that if he had wanted to, I would have even let him make love to me right there on the dance floor.

"Now, now, Katie." He pulled away from me with lust-filled eyes. "This isn't the place."

"Let's go then." I grabbed his hand without thinking and pulled him off of the dance floor. "Let's go back to your place." His eyes grew dark with desire at my words as he pushed me against the wall and ran his fingers down my neck. He stared into my eyes with such intensity that it was all I could do to not reach over and touch him.

"Are you sure you want to do that?" He growled into my ear. "Because if I take you tonight, there will be no letting go. No turning back. I will make you mine. I will possess you."

"I want you to take me." I swallowed hard at his words.

"I want you so bad, Katie." He shook his head as if to clear his mind. "Ever since the morning after I took you home, I've wanted you."

"So then take me."

"We don't have to do this if you're not ready."

I laughed then. Big, happy, and immature laughs. "Of course I'm ready. I've practically been begging you for the last ten minutes."

"Then let's go." He grabbed my hand and pulled me out of the club. We ran like school kids down the road to his apartment. Both of us aching to touch and be touched by each other. It was only when we got to his apartment door that I really stopped to think about what I was about to do. I was about to lose my virginity to a guy I had known for two weeks. Was I a slut? Was I doing the right thing? But my thoughts quickly dissipated as he picked me up, carried me into the apartment, and plopped me down on the bed.

"Would you like some wine or champagne?" He grinned down at me, and he looked like a wolf as I stared up at him. A sexy, devilish, and powerful wolf. I shook my head slowly and stared up at him, wondering if I should tell him this was my first time. It took me all of three seconds to shoot down the idea. I knew he thought I was quaint and that I wasn't used to big city ways because I was from a small town in

Florida, but I knew it wouldn't be as believable that I was a virgin. I couldn't imagine he came across many twenty-two-year-old virgins.

He started to unbutton his shirt and I stared up at him with desire pouring out of every part of my body. I gazed up at him in admiration as he threw his shirt onto the floor. His chest was well-built, with a small spattering of hair, and his six-pack looked like something from a fitness magazine. He fell down onto the bed next to me, and I reached over and lightly ran my fingers along his chest, grazing his nipples. He gasped at my touch and rolled over on top of me.

"You're wearing too many clothes," he growled, his eyes dark and intense. "Sit up." He pulled me up and I lifted my hands up so that he could pull my top off. His fingers gently went to my back and unclasped my bra before he threw it onto the floor along with my top. "Oh, Katie," he groaned before pushing me back onto the bed.

His lips immediately fell to my right breast as his fingers played with my left one. I gasped as he took my nipple in his mouth and gently nibbled on it as he sucked. He sucked as if his life depended on it, and I felt my body trembling underneath him as moisture filled my panties. I reached my hands around to his back and ran my fingers up and down, squeezing his shoulders tightly as his lips moved away from my right breast. I moaned as his lips clasped down on my left breast and my legs reached up to encircle him.

"Oh, Katie," he moaned again as he kissed up my chest and neck and back to my lips. "You taste so sweet," he muttered against my lips as his tongue found sanctuary in my mouth again. "Do you taste as sweet everywhere?"

"Everywhere?" I answered him, not thinking. All I wanted to do was feel him against me, inside of me. My body had never felt so alive before.

"Hmm, yes, everywhere." His lips left mine as he kissed back down my body, stopping at the top of my jeans for a few moments as his hands undid the button and pulled them off of me. I lay there in just my panties gazing up at him, not sure what he was going to do next. I didn't have to wait long to find out. His fingers traced an invisible line up my leg and only stopped once they reached my panties. I held my breath as his fingers ran right down the middle of my panties and circled me. I gasped and squirmed on the bed as he teased me.

"Please, Brandon," I groaned. I wanted—no I needed—to feel more of him. I needed to feel him closer, his skin against mine.

"Shh." He smiled at me and slipped his fingers into the side of my panties and rubbed my wetness. "Oh, Katie," he groaned as I continued squirming. "You are so wet for me."

"I want you," I groaned as I reached up to him, wanting to feel his chest against mine. "Let me touch you."

"Not yet." He slipped his fingers out of my panties and then pulled them down slowly and agonizingly. Every second felt like an eternity, and all I wanted was to feel his warmth against me again. I cried out when he lowered his mouth to my pussy and sucked on my bud. And then I screamed when his tongue entered me, slowly and deeply, pushing me to cliffs I never knew had existed. My fingers grabbed the sheets as his tongue continued to enter me, and I felt like I was going to die of pleasure. Waves of ecstasy took over my body so that all I could think about was the pleasure rolling through my body. "Come for me, Katie," he muttered against my pussy, and the feel of his breath against me was another new and exciting sensation. "Come for me."

"I-I can't," I groaned, shaking my head. I had never felt this way before and I was afraid that my bladder was going to burst if he kept on. "Please." I groaned as his hands spread my legs wider and he licked and sucked me with more intensity.

This time when his tongue entered me, I couldn't control it, and my orgasm exploded, sending ripple effects down my body.

"Oh, Brandon!" I screamed as my body trembled under him. He continued his exploration and his tongue lapped me up eagerly before he returned back up to kiss me.

"You taste even sweeter down there." He grinned at me before his mouth descended onto mine again. I could taste myself on his lips, and I moaned as his fingers worked their way back down my stomach and to my sweet spot. I reached my hands down to his slacks, wanting to pull them down and touch him. He laughed as I fumbled around with his button, jumped up, and pulled them off along with his boxers.

I stared at him in amazement. His cock looked like a warrior—thick, strong and firm. I swallowed as I imagined it inside of me. He looked bigger than I had imagined from photos I'd seen online with friends. I reached over and touched him softly, and he groaned as my fingers slowly worked their way up and down his shaft. I squeezed the tip of his cock and he pushed me back down on the bed.

"If you keep teasing me, Katie, I'm going to come a lot faster than I want for our first time together."

"I don't mind." I shook my head and giggled as he growled against my neck.

"I'm going to make you forget all your other lovers. I'm going to make sure that mine is the only face you think of when you think of making love. I want your body to remember me and only me."

"Okay," I gasped and closed my eyes as his fingers played with me again and his tongue tasted the lines of my neck. My hands grabbed his ass and I tried to push him toward me so that I could feel him against me.

"Oh, Katie. I need to enter you," he groaned against me ear. "Tell me you're on the pill."

"No." My eyes popped up and I bit my lower lip. "I'm not, uh, on the pill."

"Damn." He looked upset as he got off of the bed. "I wanted to feel all of you. I wanted to feel your skin against my skin, but it's fine. I have some condoms."

"Oh." I watched as he opened the drawer on his nightstand and pulled out a big box. "Did you get them because of me?"

"No." He chuckled as he pulled two out and placed one on the top of the stand. "I make sure to keep a supply."

"Oh." I looked away from him, jealousy filling me.

"You're not upset, are you?" His eyes peered at me. "You can't think I don't have sex?"
"I didn't know you were sleeping around."
"I haven't slept with anyone since I've met you."
"That was two weeks ago."
"I'm not a monk, Katie." He sat on the bed. "I like sex. We're adults. It's not a crime."
"I know." I nodded.
"If it makes you feel better, I don't want to sleep with anyone else." He smiled and kissed me hard. "I know we've only been seeing each other for two weeks, but let's see how it goes. I think we could have something special."
"Okay." I nodded again, feeling slightly happier.
"So we agree not to sleep with anyone else, right?"
"Right." I nodded a third time and he kissed me hard.
He ripped open the condom packet and quickly slid it onto his cock before lowering himself down onto me, allowing his chest to crush down on my breasts.
"Wrap your legs around my waist," he commanded me and I did so eagerly. I felt the tip of his cock at my entrance and gasped, waiting for him to finally enter me. "Oh, God, you're so wet," he groaned as he slowly entered me. I felt myself contract against him as he entered me, and for one brief second, I was scared that it was going to hurt. "Oh, Katie," he groaned as he started moving his body slowly. His cock pushed into me hard and I cried out as I felt a brief shot of pain. He looked at me with a confused and dazed look in his eyes, so I closed mine and moved underneath him.
"Fuck me, Brandon!" I cried out, and he continued moving and increasing his speed until he was sliding in and out of me smoothly. I held on to him tightly as our bodies danced to their own rhythm. My breasts bounced against his chest and his hands clasped mine as he continued making my body his.
"Open your eyes." His voice was commanding, and I opened them slowly and saw him staring into mine. "I want to see your expression as we come together." He continued moving against me and I felt like I was about to explode when his

body started shuddering and he groaned out. I climaxed then, and I held him tight to me as our bodies quaked together before he fell down on top of me. He rolled over to the right and gave me a lazy smile after a few minutes.

"That was amazing." His fingers traced the lines around my nipples as he slowly withdrew his cock from me and slipped the condom off. "Are you a virgin, Katie?" He looked up at me slowly, a question in his eyes.

"No." I shook my head.

"Really? I could have sworn you were a virgin by the way you reacted when I entered you, and I felt like I was breaking through your hymen."

"You asked if I am, but I'm not any longer." I smiled up at him and leaned over to kiss his lips. My body was tired and satiated and there was nothing that was going to ruin this moment for me.

"Ah, you tricky girl." He laughed and then sighed as he pulled me toward him. "Why didn't you tell me?"

"I didn't want you to think I was." I bit my lip.

"Oh, Katie," he whispered against my hair. "Thank you for allowing me to make love to you. I hope it was all you had hoped for."

"It was better than I had hoped for," I mumbled, and his eyes lit up with pride as he lay back with me cuddled into him.

"I'm so glad that I met you, Katie Raymond."

"Me too, Brandon Hastings." I kissed his chest and we both fell asleep.

"Excuse me, ma'am, are you lost?" The front desk clerk walked toward the elevator and stared at me.

"Sorry, what?"

"It's just that you've ridden up and down in the elevator for the last ten minutes."

"Oh, sorry." I blushed. "The purple lights just made me remember something."

"Okay." The lady gave me a strange look. "You're on the sixth floor, if you forgot."

"Yeah, thanks." I pressed the button again and shook my head. "Focus, Katie, focus," I mumbled to myself. Now was not the time to relive my memories of Brandon Hastings. He hated me and I hated him, and I was praying that if he saw me he wouldn't remember who I was. It didn't matter how great it had been when we first started dating. It didn't matter that his touch made my whole body melt. It was over. He had broken my heart, and if I wasn't careful, he was going to ruin my business career as well.

I walked out of the purple-lit elevator and to my room reluctantly. I didn't want to be here. I didn't want to be reminded of Brandon. Not now. Not when everything in my life was finally getting better. I had even started dating a new guy just before I got the job. He was a nice guy as well. Matt was someone I could see myself with in a serious relationship. He was safe and I knew he really liked me; it didn't matter that he didn't set my heart on fire like Brandon had. I was older and wiser now. I knew what real love was. What Brandon and I'd had was a fantasy—a fantasy built on lies—and when it all came crashing down, it had nearly broken me. I wasn't going to let myself dwell on the past. I couldn't allow myself to go down that road again.

***

The alarm went off at five a.m. and I wanted to roll over and go back to sleep again. "Get up, Katie," I lectured myself as I pulled the blankets up over me. I groaned and sat up, adjusting my eyes to the darkness.

I got out of bed and turned on the light and opened my suitcase. Meg and I had gone shopping before the trip, and I had gotten the sexiest business attire I could find. I had also gotten some new makeup, new perfume, and a new Chi straightener so that my hair would be as sleek as possible. I wanted to make sure I looked as good as I had ever looked. I didn't want him to recognize me, but if he did, I wanted to look as hot and sexy as possible.

I grabbed my shower cap and walked to the bathroom. I needed to shower first, and then I would do my hair. I stared at my wild waves in the bathroom mirror and groaned. It was going to take at least an hour to get my hair anything close to straight and sleek. I stared at my appearance again and started laughing as I thought about going to work looking like this. Brandon would definitely remember me if I turned up like this.

***

"Let's shower together." Brandon pulled me out of bed with him the night after we made love for the first time.
"I'm still tired," I mumbled.
"There's time to sleep tonight."
"Not if you wake me up a million times tonight like you did last night."
"Well, I need to get as much of you as I can while you're here."
"I'll be here next weekend." I yawned and stretched.
"I'd love it if you stayed here this week as well."
"What?" I froze and looked at him with wide eyes.
"I know, I know. I'm moving too fast. Sorry, I've just never felt this way before."
"Oh." I jumped out of bed and kissed him. "I've never felt this way before either."
"I just want to spend every night with you."
"I know." I sighed. "But I need to stay at my own place. It's just easier for me to get to work from there."
"I guess I could spend a couple of nights there if you want."
"No!" I shouted and then stepped back. "Sorry, it's a mess and I'd be embarrassed for you to see it."
"Don't be embarrassed." He pulled me toward him and kissed me. "I'm sure you have lots of debt from college, and I'm sure your new job can't be paying you that much. I don't care where you live."
"Uh, thanks." I buried my face into his chest, shame turning my face red. "It's hard as a new grad, you know, especially in this economy."

"Where did you go to school again?" He questioned me.
"Columbia... Uh, I mean, I always wanted to go to Columbia. I went to Florida Atlantic University," I mumbled, wanting to die.
"I'm always looking for new account managers for the hedge fund, if you're interested in doing stocks?"
"Oh, thanks, but I couldn't." I smiled weakly. "It wouldn't be right. We only just started dating. I don't want you to think I'm taking advantage of you."
"I know." He kissed the top of my head. "I think that's why I like you so much. You're the furthest thing from a gold digger I've met in New York."
"Well, you would know," I said, quite surly, and he laughed.
"Don't be jealous, Katie."
"I'm not," I pouted and followed him into the bathroom. "Oh my God, look at my hair!" I cried out as I looked into the mirror and saw a crazy mess. "I look awful."
"No, you don't. You look beautiful." He walked up behind me and put his arms around my waist. "Though I can check to see if there are any lost birds."
"Lost birds?" I wiggled against him as I looked back at him.
"You know, that thought your hair was a nest."
"Jerk." I laughed as he picked me up and placed me on the vanity.
"I can be a jerk if you want."
"Oh?" I pulled him toward me and felt his hardening cock against my leg.
"Yeah, I can do this." He placed the tip of his cock against my pussy and pushed it in slightly so that the tip was inside me. "And I can do this." He slowly entered me and I moaned as I felt him inside me. "And then I can do this." He withdrew from me and I whimpered as he left my body.
"Brandon," I groaned and he laughed.
"I told you I can be a jerk."
I squeezed my legs around him and tried to pull him into me again but he laughed.
"Not so fast, young lady."
"Make love to me," I groaned as I reached up to kiss him.

“I don’t have a condom on me.” He shrugged and I let out a light groan, disappointed. “You should get on the pill.”
“Huh?” I bit down into his shoulder, distracted by his musk.
“You should go to the doctor and get on the pill.”
“Oh, okay,” I murmured as I ran my fingers down his abs.
“Do you have health insurance at your job? Do you need me to take you to my doctor?”
“I have health insurance.” I licked down his chest as he fondled my breasts. “I’ll go in on Monday.” I would have to look online to see what time the university health center opened. I cringed as I thought about having to tell the nurse why I was there. But I figured they should be happy I was having safe sex. This wasn’t my high school anymore. I wasn’t going to get a lecture about abstinence.
“I wish you were on it now,” he whispered in my ear. “I want to take you right here and feel your pussy walls close in on my cock as I take you on a journey you've never even imagined.”
“So why don’t you?” I gasped, willing him to enter me.
“I don’t want to get you pregnant.” He chuckled and stared at me seriously. “I’m not really a guy that’s done relationships, and this is new to me. I don’t want to mess anything up.”
“You won’t.” I took his face in my hands and kissed him softly. “You won’t mess anything up,” I whispered against my lips and my heart fluttered as he carried me back to the bedroom and to his bed.
I had been right as well. He hadn’t messed anything up. I had.

***

Fisherman’s Wharf was not full of fishermen. Or at least it wasn’t when I arrived. I walked around for a little bit, glad that it wasn’t hot and humid. Hot and humid meant my perfectly coiffed hair would be a frizzy mess in minutes. Once it hit eight a.m., I walked into the building that Marathon Corps’s company-wide orientation was going to be in and looked around for a welcome table. I saw it right away, and I gasped as I walked toward it. The table was decorated with white orchids, and I couldn't not think of the night I'd realized that I'd loved him. Every time I saw orchids, I thought of Brandon. Even Meg knew never to bring them into the apartment we shared. Every time I saw them, I cried. Even now, I felt teary eyed. I took a deep breath and continued toward the table. I couldn't afford to get emotional now. Not now. Not when my makeup looked so perfect. It didn't matter that my heart was beating in my stomach and all my senses were in high alert. It didn't matter that there were orchids there. It meant nothing, absolutely nothing.

Brandon and I had seen each other every weekend for the first two months of our dating. He had asked to come over to my apartment several times but seemed to accept the fact that I'd been too embarrassed to have him in my apartment. We saw each other some weeknights as well, but he seemed to like the fact that I didn't ask to see him every day. I gave him his space. I didn't call or text him every few hours, and I didn't check up on him. He didn't know that I didn't have time to check on him. I was in classes or the library most days, and phones were banned from both. I had to study in the daytime because I knew I wouldn't have any time on the weekends and rarely in the evenings. He just thought I was comfortable and secure in the relationship. I was too naïve to even think that there was anything to worry about. To me, he was just Brandon, a handsome man I was dating, but to the rest of New York, he was one of the most eligible bachelors in the city.

"Can you come over tonight?" I glanced at the text as I walked to my next class. It was a Wednesday, and I had an English test the next day.

"I think so," I texted back quickly and happily.

"Can you take the day off of work tomorrow?"

"Don't think so. You know Maggie," I texted back quickly. Maggie was my fictional boss. Meg and I had spent an entire night creating a fake company and job for me. Maggie was my bitch of a boss who hated me and made me work late a lot.

"I wish you would quit that job and come and work for me. ;) ;)" I laughed at his text.
"You know we wouldn't get much work done."
"I want you right now," he texted back. "I want to bend you over my desk and take you right now."
"Maybe one day."
"Shit, I'm going to have to lock my door."
"Uh oh, why?"
"I'm going to have to take care of business and I don't want my secretary to walk in."
"Wish I was there."
"So do I. So can you come over tonight?"
"I'll try to get out of work early." I bit my lip as I typed that. I knew that I needed to study, but I really wanted to see him as well.
"Great. I'll see you at 6. Don't eat. We can get take out."
"Okay, see you at 6." I hurried into the class, looked down at my jeans and t-shirt, and sighed. I'd have to go home, change into some more professional clothes, and then hurry to catch the train by five. There would be no time for me to try and study for an hour before I left.
I arrived at Brandon's place at about 6:30 p.m. and he pulled me into his arms as soon as he opened the door.
"I missed you." He kissed me and stared at my face.
"You saw me on Sunday."
"That was too long ago."
"Oh, Brandon." I squeezed his hand and walked into the apartment.
"I want you to move in with me." He grabbed me from behind and pulled me toward him again. "I want you to wake up next to me every morning."
"I told you, I can't. I have a lease." I giggled as he kissed my neck.
"I'll pay the lease off," he groaned and then walked away and into the kitchen. "I have something for you." He walked back toward me with an orchid plant.
"What's this?"
"It's an orchid plant."

"Thank you." I smiled and took it from him. "It's beautiful."
"Where would you like to put it?"
"Huh?"
"It's your housewarming gift."
"Housewarming?"
"This is your new home."
"But—"
"But nothing." He shook his head seriously. "I told you the night we made love that you're mine now."
"I…" I swallowed hard, feeling the intensity of his emotions reverberating off of his body.
"You're the only woman I've ever asked to live with me." He grabbed my hands. "I thought you'd be happy."
"I am. It just seems so fast."
"Is it my age?" He sighed and my heart quickened.
"What?" I stammered. Did he know?
"I know I'm thirty-five and you're in your early twenties. I know there is more of the world you want to see and explore. I don't want to be selfish, but you're special. You're someone I could spend the rest of my life with."
"Do you think I'm too young for you?" I bit my lip and he laughed.
"If anyone would have asked me how young I would date, I never would have said twenty-two before I met you."
"Oh." I smiled weakly. "And now?"
"And now, I don't think age matters."
"So you'd date someone younger than twenty-two?"
"Oh, hell no." He laughed. "I have a reputation. I'd have nothing in common with someone younger."
"I see."
"So you're mine now, Katie." He gazed deep into my eyes. "Move in with me and let me spoil you." I kissed him then because I didn't know what to say. How could I tell him that I lived in a dorm on campus? How could I tell him that I was eighteen and that there was no way in hell my parents would approve of me cohabitating with a man almost twice my age? A man who had taken my virginity. A man they had never met!

"So, where shall we put the orchid?"
"In the kitchen, by the window." I pulled away from him slowly. "They like light."
"Good idea." He reached into his pocket and smiled at me. "I have something else for you."
My face went white as I saw him pulling his hand out... *Oh God,* I thought, *he's going to propose.*
"Here is a set of keys."
"Keys?" I looked at him blankly and then laughed as I realized what they were for. "Oh, thank you."
"Now, let's go to bed."
"To bed?"
"I need to have you now. I've been dreaming of making love to you since you left."
"Oh, I thought we were going to eat?"
"You want to eat?" He looked incredulous.
"I'm a bit hungry." I nodded and then my stomach growled. His eyes crinkled and he laughed heartily before he grabbed me up and swung me around.
"Then eat you shall." He kissed my forehead and put me back down. "I love you, Katie," he whispered into my ear. I melted against him and passionately kissed him back. It was the first time he had said those words to me, and it gave me a heady feeling. I stared at the orchids and smiled as his hands rubbed my back. The orchids signaled a change in our relationship—a change I was excited about, even if I wasn't quite sure how everything was going to work out.
"Are you here for the orientation?" a sharp voice questioned me, and I looked up with a tight smile.
"Yes, I am. Katie Raymond from the New York office."
"Okay, let me find your packet." The lady looked back at me with glassy blue eyes, her red hair cut in a sharp bob. She had a nametag on that read Priscilla and I thought the name suited her. A bitchy name for a bitchy-looking person.
"Here." She roughly handed me a folder. "Walk down the hallway to the elevator, go up to the tenth floor, and get out. You'll see the signs to show you to your first meeting."

"Thanks," I nodded and was about to say more, but she was already speaking to the person behind me. I walked to the elevator uncertainly, feeling out of place. I didn't fit in here. Sometimes I wondered if I was cut out for the business world.

I waited a few minutes for the elevator and walked in slowly. Part of me wanted to run out, catch a plane back home, and just look for another job. I didn't even bother looking up when the elevator stopped at the next floor.

I was debating whether I should just go home when I realized that whoever had entered the elevator hadn't pressed a button. It was then that I looked up. It was then that my life flashed before my eyes. I fell back against the wall as I stared into his face. He looked different, but he also looked the same. Everything about this moment was so much worse and so much more powerful than I had imagined it would be.

"Hello, Katie."

"Hello, Brandon," I whispered and stared at his face, trying to memorize every line and hair for future reference. He took a step toward me, and his hands rested on my shoulders. I swallowed hard and looked up so that our eyes were connected. Then he leaned in and pressed his lips against mine softly.

"That's for the memories," he whispered, and I smiled at him weakly, tears filling my eyes. I couldn't believe he'd remembered that line. It had been so many years since he'd first said it.

Chapter 3

"That's for the memories." Brandon pushed me against the elevator wall as soon as the door closed.
"What memories?" I stared at him, wide-eyed.
"The ones we're about to make."
"Huh?"
"Shh!" He placed a finger against my lips. "If you make noise, people may hear."
"Hear what?" I stared at the glint in his eyes. "Brandon, what are you thinking?"
"You know how I've always dreamed of office sex?"
"Uh huh."
"So, we're about to have some."
"We're not in the office." I shook my head and then his meaning dawned on me. "What if someone comes in?" I looked at the doorway in a panic.
"No one will come in." He grinned. "I put a sign on the doors, and we're stopped right now."
"Oh my God, Brandon." My face went bright red. "I don't know about this."
"I'm a bad influence, aren't I?" He bent down and sucked on my neck. "But I just want to have you everywhere."
"You can have me everywhere in the apartment." I laughed. "Everywhere and anywhere."
"Now that we live together, that's not so much fun." His fingers ran up my shirt. "That's safe sex."
"I thought you were all about safe sex." I raised an eyebrow at him and he growled as his fingers slipped under my bra and squeezed my nipples. "Oh," I moaned.
"You know you want to." He unbuttoned my shirt, bent his head, and took my nipple in his mouth.
"Oh, Brandon," I moaned and my hands squeezed his arm muscles. "How can I say no?"
"You can't. You're just as insatiable as I am," he growled as his hand slipped in between my legs. "I'm glad you wore a skirt today."

"You chose my outfit." I rolled my eyes at him.
"Well, I wanted to see you in your new skirt."
"Uh huh."
"And your new thong." He licked his lips and I laughed, not quite believing how different my life was right now. I had been 'living' with Brandon now for two weeks and it was working out quite well. We had a rule where we kept work at work, so I didn't have to discuss what was going on in the *office* if I didn't want to. Brandon had been aghast when I had moved in with one lonely suitcase. I'd made some excuse up about my not having much stuff, which was true—all the furniture belonged to Columbia University. He'd felt so bad for me that he had taken me shopping and showered me with clothes and underwear. I felt a bit like Julia Roberts in *Pretty Woman*, only I didn't mind. He was my boyfriend, not my john, and he loved me. It was all okay if he loved me. I mean, I could see it in his eyes and hear it in his voice. I'd never felt so special before, so loved. It almost made me wonder why I had put so much time and effort into my studies in high school when I could have been dating and having fun. Wasn't this what life was about? Living and feeling? Not just reading and researching all day. Though I knew Meg and the others were deeply concerned about the direction in which my life was going.
"It's not a good idea, Katie." Meg had begged me to rethink moving in with Brandon.
"I'll still be your roommate too, technically." I'd sighed. "Don't worry. You'll still see me all the time."
"I don't know, Katie."
"He's a nice guy, Meg."
"Well, I've never met him, so how would I know?" I'd left then, because what could I say? She knew why she had never met him. All of my friends knew why. I wasn't a liar. Well, only with him.
"You're wet already," he growled as his fingers slipped between my legs.
"Well, how can I not be?" I pushed him back into the side panel of the elevator and kissed him hard. He groaned as

my hands fell to his belt buckle and undid it smoothly. I was now a pro at getting him undone in record time.

"I love it when you take charge."

"I love it when you want us to make memories," I laughed as I unzipped him and kissed my way down his shirt before falling onto my knees and taking him into my mouth. I felt heady with power as he groaned and pulled my hair as I bobbed up and down on him. The salty taste of him growing in my mouth turned me on even more and I took him into my mouth faster and more eagerly.

"Slow down, Katie," Brandon groaned. "I'm going to come if you keep this up."

"That's the idea." I laughed and took him into my mouth as far as I could go. Brandon was the first and only man I'd ever given a blowjob. He was the first of many things. He only knew about the sex though. I wasn't sure how he'd feel if he knew just how inexperienced I had been previous to meeting him. I tried to blank that out of my mind, though the guilt was making everything harder and harder.

He called out my name as he orgasmed into my mouth. I swallowed without thinking, wanting to taste all of him, enjoying the feel of his release as it smoothly slid down my throat.

"Oh how I love you, Katie." He pulled me up and turned me around, bending me over and pushing my thong to the side as his fingers slowly entered me. "Oh, you're so ready for me." He grunted as his fingers roughly made love to me. "I can never get enough of you." He groaned and removed his fingers quickly. I moaned in response, and before I knew it, he was sliding into me fast and deep.

"You're hard again already?" I cried out in surprise and gratification.

"I just have to look at you to be hard, Katie." He grunted as he held on to my hips. His hands swung me around and reached up to squeeze my breasts. "Hold on to the wall. I don't want you to fall."

"Fall?" I questioned between gasps, but I soon realized what he was talking about as he slid in and out of me with such force and intensity that I could barely stand still. "Oh Brandon!" I screamed as his cock fell out of me. "Don't stop."

"I'm not going to." His cock entered me again, and this time he moved in and out so slowly that I thought time was standing still. My nerve endings felt like they were going to explode, and I wiggled my ass to try and get him to move faster again. I needed to feel him deep inside of me. I needed him to consume and take me. I needed to have him possess every inch of my body and soul.

I gripped the wall and closed my eyes as he took me in the elevator. I screamed as he increased his pace and my body started trembling as my orgasm built up.

"Come for me, Katie," he groaned. "Come for me."

"I'm close," I whimpered. My hips buckled underneath him as his fingers reached around and played with my clit while he continued his dominance over my body. "Oh Brandon!" I screamed." I'm coming, I'm coming." I screamed as my body shuddered and he continued fucking me. I banged my hands against the wall and hit something. Before I knew what was happening, the elevator started moving.

"Oh shit, Katie. What did you do?" he groaned as he continued sliding in and out of me.

"I don't know!" I screamed again as the orgasm took over my body. I couldn't think about anything other than the pleasure that was reverberating through me. "Oh, Brandon, I love you!" I cried out in ecstasy. And then the elevator stopped.

What happened next was most probably one of the most exciting, exhilarating, and scary parts of my life. Brandon grabbed me and pulled me to the corner of the elevator with him. He pushed the front of my skirt down and handed me his briefcase to hold. Seconds later, the door opened and two men walked in.

"Good afternoon, Mr. Hastings." They nodded and smiled at him.

"Mark. Jason." He smiled at them before they pressed their floor buttons and faced the front.

"Don't say a word," Brandon whispered in my ear. I stifled a gasp as I felt him push me forward slightly and slip his cock back inside of me. He moved slowly, not wanting to draw any attention to us.

"What are you doing?" I gasped as I whispered back to him.

"I'm going to come again." He winked at me. "And I think we'd all I rather come in you than in my hands and on the floor."

"Oh, Brandon." I shook my head.

"Just move back a little bit to meet me," he whispered. "Yes, keep moving your hips like that. Oh yes." His fingers dug into my hips, and I pretended to stare at something on the ground as I felt his body trembling behind me.

One of the men turned around. "You heard Pepsi shot up two hundred points, right, Brandon?"

"Yeah." His voice was rough, and I smiled.

"Your dad was happy, said if it keeps up we'll all have big bonuses this year."

"That would be nice," Brandon grunted as his fingers tightened their grip. A devious thought crossed my mind and I started humming and gyrating.

"What are you doing?" Brandon asked casually as the guy stared at us both.

"Nothing. Just dancing to the music in my head."

"I see." His eyes glinted at me and I smiled at him.

"Do you work here?" The guy gave me a friendly look. "I've never seen you before."

"I'm Katie." I smiled at him and shook his head. "I'm a friend of Brandon's."

"She's my girlfriend," Brandon mumbled, and I noticed the guy's surprised look.

"Oh." He turned back around and Brandon pulled me back so that I was right against him. I felt his body shuddering as his cock slid in and out of me quickly. He let out a slight groan and then I felt an explosion of warm semen fill me up as he orgasmed in me.

"This is our stop. See you later." The guy nodded as they exited the elevator, and neither Brandon nor I responded.

"Do you think they knew?" I gasped as Brandon turned me around and kissed me hard. He brushed the back of my skirt down and quickly zipped up his pants.
"Who knows? Who cares?" He laughed and grabbed my hand.
"I guess not you."
"Why should I care? This is the best elevator ride I've ever had." He laughed and kissed my cheek. "I don't know how I got so lucky."
"I don't know how either," I joked, and his eyes grew serious.
"I think you may very well be the one, Katie Raymond. You may very well be the one."

"So how have you been?" Brandon asked me softly at the same time I mumbled, "Fancy seeing you here." He chuckled and I blushed.
"I'm good. How are you?" I spoke softly, scared that he could hear my rapidly beating heart. My eyes took in his appearance greedily. He looked even more handsome than I remembered, but just as smart in his dark grey suit. His hair looked as black as ever, and it was still moist from his morning shower. He hadn't shaved this morning—I could tell from the light stubble around his chin—and I clenched my hands to stop myself from rubbing my fingers over it. This elevator ride was so much different than the elevator ride we'd had so many years ago.
"Great." He rubbed his lips. "Sorry about the kiss. I forgot for a moment."
"It's fine." I blushed, not needing to ask what he had forgotten.
"You look well." He looked me over quickly and disinterestedly. I felt disappointed that he hadn't studied my body a little longer—or my face—but I guess he just didn't care.
"Thank you. So do you," I spoke disjointedly, and it felt weird being so polite with someone who knew every intimate part of my body

"You still look bright-eyed and bushy-tailed." He smiled at me, but it didn't reach his eyes. "I guess you'll always have a youthful look."

"Yes, I guess so." I turned my face away, heat flooding my face at his unsubtle comments.

"So you work for Marathon Corp?" he asked me casually as we exited the elevator.

"Yes, yes I do."

"I take it the resume wasn't faked?" He raised an eyebrow and I stared at him blankly. This was going to be harder than I thought.

"Everything on my resume was true."

"It's a good thing it's illegal to ask for someone's age when hiring them, isn't it?" He looked at me coldly and I shivered. All pretense was gone from his demeanor. He still hated me. He still hadn't forgiven me.

"I made a mistake once." I looked him directly in the eye. "I've never done it again."

"That's good to hear. Or is that another lie?"

"I didn't mean to lie." I repeated the words I had cried to him so many times in the past.

"If it had only been one small lie and you had told me the truth, then I would have understood. But you perpetuated a fabrication of your life." He stared at me with a hostile expression as his words tore into my soul. "Everything was a lie."

"It wasn't all a lie." I bit my lip. *I did love you*, I wanted to scream at him. *I did love you and you were supposed to love me. You were supposed to forgive me*. But I kept quiet.

"You'd still be lying if I hadn't caught you." He shook his head furiously. "It was all just a game for you, wasn't it? A high school girl caught up in a high school game."

"I wasn't in high school."

"Close enough." He looked away from me. "What difference does a couple of months make?"

I remained silent, not knowing what to say. He was right, of course. I hadn't known when or how I was going to tell him the truth. Of course I had felt guilty. I'd felt extremely guilty.

Especially when he'd asked to meet my friends and family. I pretended I'd fallen out with the girls I'd gone to Doug's with that first night and that I hadn't made any new friends yet. Family had been easy to discuss as they were all in Florida. I'd told him that one day we could make a trip for him to meet them and he had been fine with that.

It had become more difficult when he asked about work, wanting to meet my colleagues and attend one of the many happy hours I'd talked about. I had joined some study groups and told him I was trying to bond with workmates. I'd used sex to shut him up every time he'd brought up the topic.

Aside from that, everything else had been going swimmingly. Neither of us was a great cook, so we had taken a gourmet cooking class together every Saturday morning and cooked dinner for each other every Saturday night before making love for hours on end. I suppose eventually that would have gotten old and we would have wanted to do more than cook and have sex, but we'd still been in the honeymoon phase of our relationship.

It had been easy for me to skip the alcohol questions. I'd told him after the hangover I'd had that first night that I didn't really want to drink much anymore, so I'd only had a few sips of wine when we were at home.

When he asked to see my driver's license picture one day, I'd told him I had lost it on the subway and was going to get a new one when I had more time. It hadn't mattered much, as I didn't drive, and we'd never spoken of it again.

Brandon loved to show me new things in the city. I was his first real girlfriend since he had left college. I tried not to think of that too much, though, as I'd always felt jealous when I thought about his ex-fiancée and the subsequent women he had bedded. I didn't like to think of him with other women. I wanted to be the only one in his life and in his memories. He laughed frequently when I asked him who he loved the most, who he thought of the most, who he wanted to be with the most. He thought it was cute that I had small insecurities about his past. He'd always kiss my forehead and tell me I was the one and only in his life, forever and always, and I would happily melt against him.

Everything was going perfectly, up until that day. I had organized my schedule so well that even I forgot that I was just an eighteen-year-old freshman at Columbia University and not an entry-level associate at a marketing firm in the city.

"I've got a work presentation tomorrow," he groaned one night as I ran my hands down to his boxer shorts. "I'm not even prepared."

"Is that your way of telling me no?" I laughed at him and kissed his nipples. "Are you really telling me no?"

"I know. Call me an old man or something. But I have to go and give a talk and I have nothing ready. I'll have to leave early in the morning to prepare and then catch a train to the Upper West Side."

"Aww." I really wasn't listening. I was too busy trying to entice him. If I'd paid better attention, instinct bells would have gone off when he'd said Upper West Side.

"I can tell that you care." He laughed and pulled me on top of him. "What's your day like tomorrow? Can you get out of work early or meet me for lunch?"

"Hmmm." I rubbed myself back and forth on him as he reached up and grabbed my breasts. "I'm not sure. I think I have a meeting." I gasped as he leaned up, took one of my nipples into his mouth, and sucked. "I can see what I can do," I moaned as I increased my pace as I dry-rubbed him. His cock was hanging out of his boxers and rubbing up against me through my panties.

"I'd love to take you to lunch, maybe even have sex in the bathroom."

"What bathroom?" I gasped as he slipped a finger into my panties and rubbed my clit.

"The restaurant bathroom," he groaned as I rubbed my breasts in his face. "I know how you love public sex."

"You mean you love it." I laughed slightly. "I'm not sure if I can tomorrow, my boss wants to have a lunch meeting with me."

"Oh no." He made a face in sympathy. "I hope everything is okay."
"Yeah, it'll be fine." I gasped as he slipped my panties to the side and guided his cock into me. "Oh, I thought you needed to sleep?"
"I'm never so tired that I can say no when my girl wants to ride me." He held my hips as I slowly bounced up and down on him. "Ride me faster, cowgirl." He moved my hips back and forth and I swiveled on top of him, letting his hard cock slide in and out of me like a bullet.
"Call me if you get out early. Maybe we can do a late lunch," he groaned, and I giggled. It was always funny to me when he tried to hold a conversation during sex.
"Will do," I gasped before I screamed. He flipped me over onto my knees and came up behind me and slipped his cock back inside of me. "Oh my!" I screamed again as he slammed into me hard. I loved it when we did it doggy style because I always seemed to feel every inch of him inside of me, hitting spots I'd never known existed before.
"Or think about quitting and coming to work for me." He grunted behind me. "Or maybe even just quit and we can start a family." His words were low and I froze for a second. I didn't respond because an orgasm took over my body and I was screaming out his name to continue fucking me. He came pretty quickly after me, and I snuggled into his arms as we settled in for sleep. I stroked his chest with my eyes closed and enjoyed the warm feeling of satisfaction that rested in me.
"I wasn't just saying that, you know," he whispered against my hair. "I know we haven't been together long and you've just started your career, but I'd really like to take this to the next level soon. I love you, Katie Raymond." I didn't respond to him and pretended that I had fallen asleep, but my heart couldn't stop pounding at his words. I was hopelessly in love with this man and yet scared at the same time. How could I marry him and have his babies when he didn't know the truth about me? Because I knew one hundred percent that he was the man I wanted to spend my life with.

I met Meg for breakfast before my first class the next day because I had nothing to prepare for class. Some top businessman was coming to give a talk about what it meant to be a leader in the business world. I wasn't really interested in hearing what he had to say, but I was glad that I had a day off from reading for class. I filled Meg in on the happenings of the night before, but she didn't look happy for me.

"Katie, I love you. I really do. You're my best friend and I know you love this man. But he's also the first guy you've ever dated. You're moving way too fast. For all you know, this is puppy love."

"It's not puppy love. I love him." I shook my head and sighed. "You just don't understand."

"Does he even know that you're going home for Christmas break?"

"No." I shook my head. "I'm thinking about calling my parents and telling them I can't come. Brandon wants me to meet his folks."

"Katie, you cannot flake out on your parents. Think how disappointed they will be. Not to mention they will be on the first flight out here, and how are you going to explain that you're now living with your older boyfriend?"

I groaned at her words. I knew she was right. I'd have to come up with an excuse to tell Brandon. Maybe I would tell him that my business lunch was me getting a promotion, but I'd have to travel abroad for the holidays.

"What are you doing?" She frowned as I whipped out my phone.

"How does this sound?" I asked her as I started texting. "Guess what, honey? I think I'm getting a promotion. There is a rumor going around the office that my boss is going to promote me. Only thing is, I may be gone for Christmas. Business travel."

"It sounds long and it sounds like a lie." Meg sighed. "Why don't you just tell him the truth?"

"I can't." I shook my head. "Not yet." I hit send and sat back. "You don't understand, Meg. I want to tell him the truth, but I'm just not sure he will understand."
"If he loves you, he will."
"I know." I closed my eyes. "I'm going to tell him after Christmas, I promise."
"Okay." She looked like she wanted to say more, but she didn't. "Did he respond?"
"Yeah," I smiled. "He said, 'Congrats. Can't wait to hear all about it. Wish me luck this morning. I can't stand having to do this talk. Love, your Brandon.'"
"Well, I guess he fell for it." Meg shook her head. "Let's get to campus. I have class in a few minutes."
"Yeah, me too. Just a boring guest lecture though." I grinned. "Maybe I can get started on my biology homework."
"You're so bad, Katie." Meg laughed at me and I shrugged. "If I sit in the back, no one will notice what I'm doing."
"Good luck with that." We hugged quickly and then parted ways outside Butler Library.
"See you for study group tomorrow?" She looked at me hopefully and I nodded.
"Of course. I need it or I'm going to fail my finals next week." We both laughed even though my words were true, and I walked to my class absentmindedly. I walked into the classroom and sat in the back row, checking my text messages before turning off my phone and putting it in my bag. I pulled out my biology textbook and started going through the checklist my study group and I had prepared for the final. The teacher started talking and introducing the speaker, but I was so engrossed in one of the charts I was making that I didn't even look up.
"Ms. Raymond, do you have something more important than today's class?" the professor called out to me, and my face went red as I looked up to apologize.
"No, sorry, Professor Wright." I offered him a small smile and then froze as I looked to the right of him. In that moment, I felt a million different emotions coursing through my body. I

honestly wanted to die or faint, but neither one of them occurred.

The smile left my face as I stared at the guest speaker. It was Brandon, and as his eyes met mine, I saw a flash of surprise, wonder, and anger in his eyes. He looked at me blankly for a moment and I offered him a small smile. He turned away from me and my heart started beating. I didn't know what to do or say. I wanted to jump up, grab his arm, and pull him out of the classroom to explain. I needed to explain to him that I hadn't been lying—not on purpose. I wanted to tell him that this was all a mistake. But I knew I couldn't and so I just sat there.

"Class, I want to introduce you to multi-billionaire Brandon Hastings. Mr. Hastings, meet the freshmen business students of Columbia University." Brandon smiled at the crowd and nodded, but his eyes sought mine. They looked shocked and angry, and I felt deeply ashamed of myself. I wanted to scream at Professor Wright for telling him we were all freshmen. I wasn't even going to be able to pretend that I was a senior. I felt immediately angry at myself for even thinking of replacing one lie with another.

The talk seemed to pass by like a flash of lightning. I was surprised because I had thought it would drag on. But somehow hearing Brandon's voice soothed me. He sounded normal, happy even, and I was able to convince myself that everything was going to be okay. But then the class ended and he walked out with the professor without even giving me a second glance.

I sat at the back of the room for about five minutes, unsure of what to say and do. I felt frozen to my seat. I was scared to leave the room and face what was to come. I didn't want to go to my study group and I didn't want to go home. I felt a tear sliding down my face as I sat there. I wanted my mom. I wanted to go home and hide in my bed and forget everything. I wanted to pretend like none of this had happened. I wanted to pretend I hadn't seen the look of anger and distrust in Brandon's eyes. I wanted to pretend that my heart didn't feel like it was cracking.

I stood up slowly and walked to the door with my heart in my mouth. I felt like my world was about to end and I didn't know how to stop it.
"Hey." Brandon was standing outside the door as I walked out.
"Hey." I smiled at him, happy to see him. For a moment I thought that everything was okay. I reached over to kiss him and he pulled away in disgust.
"No." He shook his head. "We need to talk."
"I'm sorry, Brandon." I rushed out. "I wanted to tell you, but I didn't know how."
"How old are you?" He looked at me and studied my face and body as if seeing me for the first time.
"Eighteen," I mumbled.
"What?"
"I'm eighteen."
"Not twenty-two?"
"No, I'm not twenty-two."
"Jesus Christ!" he exclaimed and then swore.
"It doesn't change how I feel about you." I reached out to touch his face and he recoiled away from me.
"It changes everything, Katie." His voice was loud. "You're a fucking freshman in college."
"I still love you."
"You don't even know what love is." He spat out the words and looked at me in disgust. "I can't believe you lied to me! You've been lying to me all this time. How could you?"
"I didn't mean to lie." I felt my eyelids getting heavy. "It's not something I intended to do."
"What was the text message all about?" He pulled out his phone. "I was going to buy you fucking flowers, Katie. I was going to buy you flowers and take you to dinner to congratulate you."
"I'm sorry." I looked down ashamed.
"So where did the promotion come from? Is it because I told you I wanted to have kids with you? Did you need to figure out a reason to get out of committing to me?"

"No, that's not it!" I cried out. "That's not why. I have to go home for Christmas," I said slowly. "My parents expect me to come home over Christmas break."
"Oh my god, your parents." His eyes looked glazed. "That's why you've never told them about me and why I've never met your friends. They don't know about me, do they?"
"They do! At least my friends do." I bit my lower lip. "I was scared for you to meet them. They all look their age."
"You mean you were worried that I would wonder why all my girlfriend's friends were eighteen and in college?" He laughed bitterly. "Or were you going to ask them to lie to me as well?"
"No, of course not." I reached for his hand. "Please, Brandon. Don't be like this. I love you."
"You love me?" He laughed a deep sorrowful sound. "You love me, huh?"
"Yes," I nodded bleakly. "I really do love you."
"Then prove it to me."
"How?"
"Fuck me."
"Huh?" I looked at him confused.
"Let's go outside and find somewhere to fuck."
"What do you mean?"
"If you love me, you will do anything I want to make me happy, right?"
"Yes, of course." I swallowed and followed him out of the building.
"Follow me." He grabbed my arm and dragged me besides him. We walked to the front of the library and then to the side of the building by the trash bins. "Pull your skirt up and bend over."
"What?" I frowned as he pushed me forward and lifted my skirt up before pulling my panties down.
"I want to fuck you."
"Here?" I looked at him like he was crazy. Anyone could walk around the corner and see us.

"Yes, here." He unzipped his pants and pulled his cock out before rubbing the tip against my opening. "Shit, you're wet already," he groaned as he slowly entered me.
"Oh, Brandon." I groaned as he filled me up.
"I love you, you know that, right, Katie?" he grunted as he pushed me toward the garbage cans. "Hold on tight. This is going to be hard and fast."
"I love you too, Brandon," I moaned, not caring in that moment if anyone heard or saw me. "Please forgive me."
"Shh." He moved faster and faster, and I gripped the garbage cans tight as he pummeled into me, letting all of his emotions out. He came hard and fast and his sperm ran down my leg as he pulled out mid-orgasm. "Oh, sorry." He looked down at the line of semen cascading down my leg.
"It's okay." I nodded and quickly pulled my panties up and my skirt down. "Can we talk?"
"I don't think so." He zipped his pants up. "I've got to get back to the office."
"Oh." I bit my lip. "We can do lunch if you want, like you said earlier."
"No." He shook his head. "I don't think so."
"Oh, maybe I can cook you dinner tonight?"
"No." He shook his head and looked at me with a blank stare. "I won't be there tonight."
"Oh?"
"I'll give you time to pack up your stuff."
"Pack up my stuff?" I frowned. "What do you mean?"
"I want you out by this weekend." He shrugged. "I'm sure it won't take long to pack up. You didn't bring much. I know why now."
"I don't want to move out." I bit my lower lip to stop myself from crying. "I love you."
"It's over, Katie."
"But I love you and you love me," I protested, trying to grab his arm and make him look at me.
"I don't date high school girls."
"I'm not in high school."

"Close enough. What difference do a couple of months really make?" He looked up at me then and stared into my eyes. "Thanks for the last fuck though. It's a better memory for me to keep than in the classroom." And then he turned around and walked away. I stood there for about thirty minutes, stunned and dazed at what had happened. Tears streamed down my face and I sat on the ground, crying as my heart broke.

Chapter 4

"I still have some of your things," Brandon continued as we walked into the large conference room.
"Oh, you could have thrown them out." I gave him a weak smile. "I'm sure none of those clothes fit me anymore."
"Yeah, perhaps not." He shrugged and looked at my figure. I felt slightly self-conscious as he looked me over. I had definitely filled out since I was eighteen. Bigger breasts, curvier figure, bigger ass. "But I didn't know if there was anything you would have wanted to keep."
"Oh, well, thanks." I glanced at his face again, unable to stop myself from studying his features. I wanted to reach over and trace the lines of his face. It felt surreal to be standing here with him. This was the first time I'd seen him since we had broken up. I'd never gone back to the apartment after he had broken up with me. I'd gone to my dorm room and cried and cried, and Meg had comforted me when she came back after her classes. I'd felt humiliated and used. Abandoned and abused, and I hated him and myself. If only I hadn't lied. Things would have been different then. That's all I could tell myself.
Every day seemed the same and I waited by the phone anxiously, willing it to ring and for it to be him, begging me to forgive him and take him back. Only he never called. And I never called him. I was too scared that he wouldn't pick up or that he would tell me that he hated me.
I held out hope for two months and then I saw a photograph of him in the *New York Post* at some function with some blonde. They were kissing, and the caption said something like *Eligible bachelor Brandon Hastings off the market*. My heart broke and I lost all hope of reconciliation. He was done with me. Forever. And there was nothing I could do.
"It is good seeing you again." He nodded. "Welcome to Marathon Corp."

"Thank you. You too." I nodded politely, as if he weren't the guy who bent me over a garbage can, fucked me, and then dumped me.

"Try to keep telling the truth." His eyes flashed at me and he walked away.

I found a seat at the table and made sure to sit away from where he was standing. I didn't want to be anywhere near him. I wanted to avoid him as much as possible. I didn't want to hear his voice or look into his eyes. I wanted to pretend that this moment wasn't happening. If I could just pretend it wasn't happening, then maybe I could ignore the stirrings of emotion in my stomach.

I sat down and eagerly leafed through the folder, pretending that it was the most interesting thing I had seen in years. I didn't make small talk with anyone and I didn't look up. Finally, a lady announced that we were all to sit down. I stayed where I was. I felt safe here. And then *he* sat next to me.

"Seat vacant?" His voice was low as he sat down next to me, and I nodded as I screamed inside. "I hope you don't mind sitting next to the big boss."

"Not at all." I faked a smile and looked away.

"Liar," he whispered, and I looked up at him in surprise. His eyes sparkled as he stared at me. "It's driving you crazy that I'm sitting here."

"No, it's not," I stuttered, and he reached his hand under the table and touched my knee."

"I can feel your legs shaking." He leaned towards me and whispered in my ear. "I'm sure if I slipped my fingers under your skirt, your panties would be wet as well."

My eyes grew wide at his words. "What?" I gasped and pushed his hand away. "What are you doing?"

"What do you think?" He cocked his head and smiled before standing up. "Welcome to the Marathon Corp management orientation, everyone. I'm your new CEO, Brandon Hastings." He looked around the room and smiled widely. "I'm happy to meet everyone this weekend and tell you the direction I see our company going in. We're going to start off with some introductions and icebreakers, thanks to Human Resources, and then we'll take a fifteen-minute break." Everyone clapped at his words and he laughed. "I don't want you all to fall in love with me too quickly. I'm a hard man to please, and as your boss, I'll be looking for your best work. I don't take excuses or lies well, so if you want to continue working here, you will all put in your best effort." Everyone was nodding in agreement at his words, and I had a worried feeling in my stomach. Was he setting everything up like this so he could fire me?

"So why don't I start first, and then the lovely lady to my left will continue." He smiled down at me graciously and I pretended to smile back at him. "My name is Brandon Hastings, and I'm in my early forties. This is the third company I've run and it likely won't be the last. I enjoy gourmet cooking—I know, I know, it's not believable, right?" He laughed. "But I took a class with an old girlfriend and I haven't been able to shake the habit—or her." He laughed again and I could feel myself blushing. "Let's see… I currently live by myself in New York City, though that may be changing soon." He gave me a look and I stared at him, wondering what his last sentence meant. "You're next."

"Okay, thanks." I stood up and took a deep breath. "Hello everyone. My name is Katie, Katie Raymond. I'm twenty-five and a graduate of Columbia and NYU. I live in New York as well, but I'm from Florida. As chance would have it, I also took a cooking class with an ex-boyfriend, but I rarely find time to cook. I guess he got all the skills." I made a face and everyone laughed except Brandon. "Let's see," I said, warming up. "I've only worked at Marathon Corp for about a month but I love it so far, so I hope that never changes. Oh, I'm in love with French movies, even though I don't speak French."

"Maybe that's something someone taught you to love?" Brandon spoke lightly, and I smiled as I nodded at him.

"Yes, someone I loved introduced me to French movies." I stared at him as I spoke and sat down. I continued to stare at him even when the man next to me started talking.

Brandon's eyes searched mine for a moment before he sighed and turned away. I felt the resolve building up in my body. I wasn't going to let him make me feel bad for what had happened. I had been young; I'd made a mistake. He couldn't hold it against me forever.

The introductions seemed to take forever, and I sat back in my chair with a fake smile on my face as I pretended to listen to what everyone was saying. I tried not to notice as Brandon's chair moved closer to mine, but there was no way to ignore the feel of his fingers as they ran up and down my leg.

"I've missed you," he leaned over and whispered in my ear. I pretended to ignore his touch and his voice and kept my face straight ahead. He pulled away from me, but his fingers continued to draw lines on my leg. I tried to shift away from him, but my movement gave him more access than I would have liked, and his fingers were able to work their way up my thigh, higher than I would have liked.

"Stop it," I finally turned my head and whispered at him.

"Stop what?" He gave me a questioning smile as his finger ran all the way up my thigh and then lightly across my panties.

"You know what," I gasped and clenched my legs. That was a mistake, because now I had trapped his hand right there. He immediately took it to his advantage and rubbed in between my legs softly. I could feel my panties growing wet before I reached down and pulled his hand out.

"That's not appropriate," I hissed at him, and he smiled.

"You didn't seem to mind before."

"That was seven years ago."

"Been counting, have we?" He raised an eyebrow and then grabbed my hand and placed it on his crotch. "You still make me hard." He left my hand there and I squeezed his cock without even thinking. It felt thick and hard, and I shifted in my seat as I thought about how much pleasure it had given me. "If you want, I'll let you go under the table and suck it." He smiled sweetly at me and I withdrew my hand quickly.

"You're an asshole," I mouthed at him.

"You made me that way," I thought he hissed back, but I wasn't sure if I had heard him correctly.

I could have dropped on my knees and thanked God when it was break time. If I had to sit there for one more minute, I might have done something I was going to regret. My head was spinning, my heart was pounding, and worst of all, I was horny as hell. I hated myself for feeling turned on by what he had done and for having daydreams of giving him a blowjob under the table as I sat there.

"Get it together," I hissed at myself as I jumped up, ran out of the room, and went to the ladies' room. I washed my face, reapplied my makeup, and just stared at my reflection. "You can do this, Katie," I repeated over and over to myself. "You only have to get through two days with him. That's it. Two days." I sighed and took a deep breath as I exited the bathroom. I groaned out loud as I saw Brandon standing there.

"Get lost, did you?"

"No."

"I'm glad you didn't fall in."

"So am I." I tried to walk past him and he grabbed my arms. "You never called."

"What?" I blinked at him.

"You never called me after that day. You never came to pick up your stuff and you never called."

"I was waiting for you to call," I said softly and stared at him. "You never called me either."

"I'm going to be working in the office with you." He'd changed the subject abruptly and I nodded.

"Okay."

"I hope it's not going to be difficult." He ran his hands through his hair. "It's not a big office. We'll likely see each other a lot."

"I'm fine. It'll be fine," I lied as my body screamed at me.

"Good." He stepped toward me and lightly pressed his body against mine. I stared up into his eyes without backing down. I wasn't going to let him intimidate me. He took another step forward, and involuntarily I stepped back and hit the wall. He

pushed up against me and I could feel his hardness against me as his breath tickled my ear.
"You feel warm."
"So do you." I stared into his eyes, not daring to breathe.
"I want to touch you." His fingers ran up my shirt. "I want to taste you again."
My body trembled under his touch, but I didn't move or say a word.
"I told you once that I would possess your body," he whispered in my ear. "I told you that I owned you. Do you remember that?"
"Yes," I squeaked out.
"Well, I want to take what's mine." His fingers squeezed my left breast as his mouth descended on mine roughly. His tongue slipped into my mouth and my back arched into him as I tasted his sweetness once again. My hands ran up his back to his hair and I caressed his silky tresses as we kissed. We both paused as we heard footsteps, and he quickly pulled me into the women's bathroom.
"Shh." He placed a finger across my lips as his eyes sparkled. He grabbed my hands, pulled me into a bathroom stall with him, and locked the door. I didn't even have time to think. He pulled my skirt up and my panties down before his fingers caressed my already wet opening. His other hand unzipped his pants and pulled his cock out, and before I could say a word, he lifted me up and pushed me against the door. "Wrap your legs around me," he growled into my ear, and I did as he said without a word.
He plunged into me and I cried out. His hand came down on my mouth and he stopped his movements.
"You have to be quiet," he whispered and I nodded. He then leaned down and kissed me again as he fucked me harder. This was not 'I missed you, let me make love to you' sex. This was 'I've worked myself up and I need to come as fast as I can' sex.
His cock plunged into me harder and harder, and I closed my eyes and squeezed his shoulders as I once again experienced the pleasure that had ruined me for other men. I

thought about Matt briefly, and a feeling of guilt swept through me. I hadn't even slept with him yet, but here I was, giving myself to Brandon. A man I hadn't seen in seven years.

"Oh yes," Brandon grunted as his body started shuddering. "Oh, yes." His movements went faster and faster and then I felt him pause. "Open your eyes, Katie."

I opened them slowly and he smiled at me, a genuine smile I hadn't seen in years.

"I want you to come first," he whispered. "I want to feel your pussy lips trembling and gushing on me when I come." He started his movements up once again, this time moving slowly. I groaned as I felt him fill me up. "I want you to come for me, Katie." He pushed against me hard. "Are you about to come?"

"Yes," I moaned as I reached the brink of an orgasm. "I'm about to come, Brandon." And then he started moving faster again and I climaxed fast and furious, my body trembling against him as he came inside of me.

"Oh, Katie." He kissed my cheek and let me down onto the ground. "I've missed you."

I straightened my skirt and looked up at him with a shy smile. "I've missed you too, Brandon." Our eyes connected for a few brief seconds before he opened the door. "I'll go out first." He ran his hands over his shirt and zipped up his pants. "You should wait a couple of minutes. We don't want to give anyone any ideas."

"Sure." I nodded uncertainly.

"I'm glad you took this job." He smiled at me and winked. "I think we're going to have a lot of fun."

"Thanks." I blushed, unsure of what to say, but a feeling of hope crept up in me. Maybe me getting this job and him becoming the CEO wasn't the worst thing in the world. Maybe—just maybe—this would work out for the best.

I waited for five minutes and then exited the bathroom. The hallways were empty, and I walked back into the conference room with a small smile on my face and a new pep in my step. I was disappointed when I sat down and Brandon wasn't there, but sat back and fluffed my hair, waiting for him to come back.

"Excuse me, everyone," the bitchy redhead from the table downstairs said as she walked back into the room. "You guys have an extended break for five more minutes. Mr. Hastings received an urgent call from his fiancée that he had to take. He'll be back soon." And then she casually walked out of the room as if her news hadn't just broken my heart again.

The End of Part I

Thank you for reading The Ex-Games Part I. This is a 3 novella erotic romance series. Part two is now available here and part three will be released on January 9th.

To be notified as soon as the next parts are released, please join the Helen Cooper Mailing List or J. S. Cooper Mailing List.

If you enjoyed this novella, please leave a review, and recommend it to a friend.

Other Books by J. S. Cooper can be found here.
Other Books by Helen Cooper can be found here.

I hope you enjoyed this book. You can like J.S. Cooper on Facebook here and Helen Cooper here.

CPSIA information can be obtained at www.ICGtesting.com
Printed in the USA
LVOW05s0008050314

376089LV00011B/332/P